Hiding

To Blair with thanks
for your wit, patience and encouragement.

Kids Can Press Ltd. acknowledges with appreciation
the assistance of the Canada Council and the Ontario Arts Council
in the production of this book.

Canadian Cataloguing in Publication Data

Aldis, Dorothy, 1896-1966
Hiding

ISBN 1-55074-103-9

I. Collins, Heather. II. Title.

PZ8.3.A43Hi 1993   j811' .52   C92-094751-4

Kids Can Press Ltd.
29 Birch Avenue
Toronto, Ontario, Canada
M4V 1E2

Designed by N.R. Jackson
Printed in Hong Kong
93 0 9 8 7 6 5 4 3

HIDING

Dorothy Aldis • Heather Collins

Kids Can Press Ltd.
Toronto

I'm hiding,

I'm hiding,

And no one knows where;

For all they can see is my

Toes and my hair.

And I just heard my father
Say to my mother-

"But, darling, he must be

Somewhere or other.

"Have you looked in the inkwell?"
And mother said, "Where?"

"In the *inkwell*," said father. But
I was not there.

Then "Wait!" cried my mother-
"I think that I see

Him under the carpet." But

It was not me.

"Inside the mirror's
A pretty good place,"

Said father and looked, but saw
Only his face.

"We've hunted," sighed mother,
"As hard as we could

And I *am* so afraid that we've

Lost him for good."

Then I laughed out aloud
And I wiggled my toes
And father said - "Look, dear,
I wonder if those

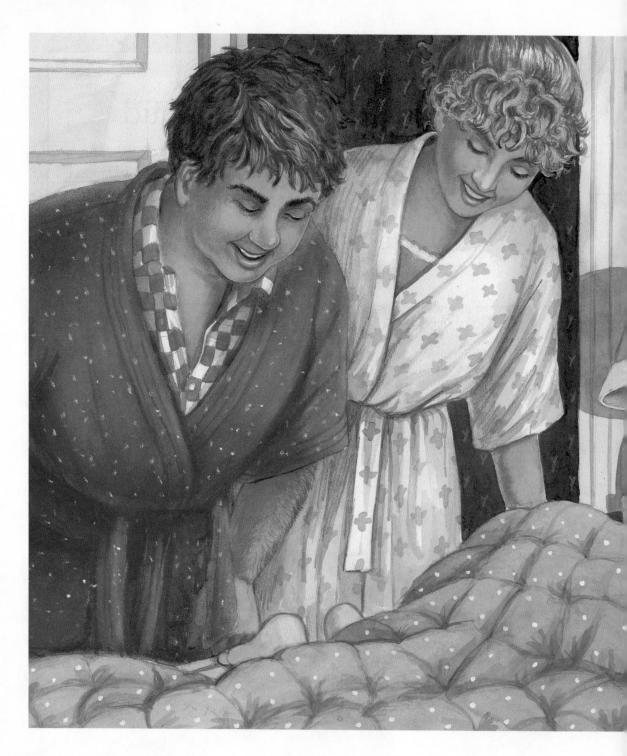

"Toes could be Benny's.

There are ten of them. See?"

And they *were* so surprised to find
Out it was me!